Don't Touch That!

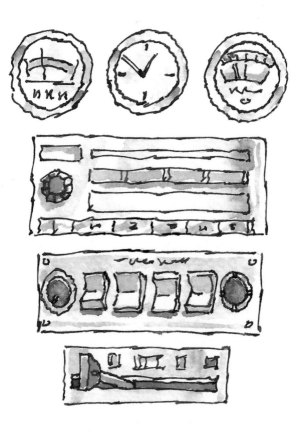

For Uncle Frank. My lost childhood Superhero and inspiration for the story. DA

For Sebastian, my super grandson! PK

Don't Touch That!

First Published in the United Kingdom in 2022 by Dan Ashton

Text copyright © Dan Ashton – January 2022
Illustrations copyright © Peter Kavanagh – January 2022
www.peterkavanagh.co.uk

Printed by Amazon Direct Print

ISBN: 979-847-497315-9

Don't Touch That!

by Dan Ashton

illustrated by Peter Kavanagh

My Dad's a **Superhero**

His Job is really cool !!

He's a superhero **teacher**

At the **superhero** school

Mum says "That is **nonsense**"
But I know that it's true
I've seen his **superhero** car
I know what it can do

He takes me for **exciting** rides
Mostly at weekends
To talk about his **missions**
With his **superhero** friends

And as he drives he shows me
All the **buttons**, all the **sockets**
"Don't touch that !!" he tells me
"That launches all the **rockets**"

We **fly** round bends and **zoom** up hills
So fast and oh so far
And **everybody** loves to see
His superhero car

"I'm not **slowing down**" says Dad
"For cyclists or learners"
And he pushes down a **pedal**

That ignites the **rocket burners**

The seats are **burnt** and **battered**

And are all **ripped** at the seams

"Battle scars" he tells me...

There's a **button** by the handbrake
That makes us **bullet proof**

It also **slides a window** back
That's fitted to the roof

"Don't touch that" he tells me
"Don't **fiddle** with those things"
When I mess with all the **levers**
That work the **jets and wings**

"One day" he says, "we'll **pull them**
And **fly** over the sea
But now it's time we went back home
For **bath time** and some **tea**"

Dad sits and reads a **story**
When I go to bed at night
A tale of **superheroes**
Meeting baddies for a fight

I close my eyes, I start to **dream**
And slowly... drift... away
Dad messes with a **lever**
"**What's this?**" I hear him say

"DON'T TOUCH THAT !!" I spring awake

"That's my **ejector** chair!"

There goes my **Super Dad**
......***flying*** through the air

Printed in Great Britain
by Amazon